Mousequerade Ball

A Counting Tale

Lori Mortensen • illustrated by Betsy Lewin

New York Times bestselling illustrator

BLOOMSBURY

NEW YORK LONDON OXFORD NEW DELHI SYDNEY

First published in the United States of America in May 2016
by Bloomsbury Children's Books
www.bloomsbury.com

Bloomsbury is a registered trademark of Bloomsbury Publishing Plc

For information about permission to reproduce selections from this book, write to
Permissions, Bloomsbury Children's Books, 1385 Broadway, New York, New York 10018
Bloomsbury books may be purchased for business or promotional use. For information on bulk purchases please contact
Macmillan Corporate and Premium Sales Department at specialmarkets@macmillan.com

Library of Congress Cataloging-in-Publication Data
Names: Mortensen, Lori, author. | Lewin, Betsy, illustrator.
Title: Mousequerade ball / by Lori Mortensen ; illustrated by Betsy Lewin.
Description: New York : Bloomsbury Children's Books, 2016.
Summary: When ten mice get dressed up for a fancy ball the arrival of a cat sends them fleeing,
but what if the cat's only intention is to dance the night away? Counting up and counting down, dancing
all the while, this delightful story invites readers to the event of the season: The Mousequerade Ball!
Identifiers: LCCN 2015022804
ISBN 978-1-61963-422-0 (hardcover) • ISBN 978-1-68119-033-4 (board)
ISBN 978-1-61963-971-3 (e-book) • ISBN 978-1-61963-972-0 (e-PDF)
Subjects: | CYAC: Stories in rhyme. | Mice—Fiction. | Cats—Fiction. |
Counting—Fiction. | BISAC: JUVENILE FICTION/Animals/Mice, Hamsters,
Guinea Pigs, etc. | JUVENILE FICTION/Performing Arts/Dance. |
JUVENILE FICTION/Animals/General.
Classification: LCC PZ8.3.M8422 Mo 2016 | DDC [E]—dc23
LC record available at http://lccn.loc.gov/2015022804

Art created with a sable brush, Winsor & Newton lamp black watercolor, and one-ply Strathmore kid finish watercolor paper
Typeset in Cheltenham and Zephyr
Book design by John Candell
Printed in China by Leo Paper Products, Heshan, Guangdong
1 3 5 7 9 10 8 6 4 2

All papers used by Bloomsbury Publishing, Inc., are natural, recyclable products made from wood grown in well-managed
forests. The manufacturing processes conform to the environmental regulations of the country of origin.

To the dancer in all of us —L. M.

To our cat, Sophie, who loves to dance
with her toy mouse —B. L.

In a castle on a hill,
in a great, grand hall,

tonight is the night
of the Mousequerade Ball.

One small mouse
lights a wee match,
puffs on the twigs
till the hot flames catch.

TWO tidy mice with a brisk whisk broom
swish, swish, swish cross the great, grand room.

Three fine mice
in black-tie suits
tighten up the strings
of their thumb-strum lutes.

Four dainty mice,
swaying to the beat,
open up their mouths
and sing real sweet.

"Sing a mousequeradey song.
Give a little squeak.
Come and dance the night away,
dancing cheek to cheek."

Five plump mice,
with a sniff and "Yum!"
slice cheddar cheese
on a fluff puff crumb.

Six eager mice
in button-down vests
open up the doors
and welcome all the guests.

Seven silly jesters do amazing tricks.

Eight grand lords twirl
their walking sticks.

Nine buccaneers tip their feathered hats.

Ten splendid ladies fan themselves
and gasp—

"CAT!"

Ten splendid ladies scatter cross the floor.

Nine buccaneers scramble out the door.

Eight grand lords scurry up the stairs.

Seven silly jesters hide behind the chairs.

Six eager mice race beneath a rug.

Five plump mice squeeze into a jug.

Four dainty mice rush
inside a sack.

Three fine mice dash
into a crack.

Two tidy mice leap
and take a chance.

One small mouse cries,
"Wait!"

"Cat has come to dance!"

Mouse does a curtsy; cat makes a bow.
They waltz round the floor, and the mice cheer——

"Wow!"

In a castle on a hill,
in a great, grand hall,
everyone's dancing
at the Mousequerade Ball.